Ben Shecter

SPARROW SONG

HARPER & ROW, PUBLISHERS

To Harriett Barton

SPARROW SONG

A soot-colored sky
covers the city.
It hangs low
and touches the empty house.
The crane
moves in.
The wrecking ball
sways,
the wrecking ball
swings,
the house trembles.

Sparrow's song
is peach-colored mornings,
in a big friendly kitchen
with organdy curtains,
strawberries, jam,
and warm buttered toast.
Sparrow's song is sweet.

Slate shingles
fall.
The roof disappears.

Hammers,
crowbars,
and fast-moving saws
pull, pry, and cut
the old house apart.
The chimney topples.
Marble mantels break.

A moonstone tub
on lion claws
moves, then later sinks
slowly
to the floor
below.

The grey mouse leaves
his cupboard
for a new home.

Crossbeams tumble,
pillars splinter.
The garden cat visits
and says,
"Hello, anyone home?"
A lunch whistle blows.
Sparrow searches for food.
There are crumbs
of cookies, cake, and bread.
Sparrow cries,
"What a treat!"

Sparrow's song is
amber afternoons
in velvet parlors
with tea in china cups,
embroidered pillows,
and lilacs in cut-glass vases.
Sparrow's song is
ginger-colored paper
in a spice-box room
smelling
of oleander, thyme, and dill.
Sparrow's song is gentle.
Sparrow's song is soft.

Dust clouds rise
behind glass windows.
Then settle
with a hissing sound
like a closetful of
snakes.
The pendulum wrecking ball
moves,
smashing,
breaking
balustrades,
banisters.
A stairway falls.

A rooftop pigeon asks Sparrow,
"What's going on here?"
"See for yourself,"
Sparrow replies.
"Too bad, too bad,"
cries the pigeon.

Cornices, moldings,
tumble down on the trellised
vines,
pulling them apart
and Sparrow's nest too.

Northpoint Elementary IMC
50800 Cherry Rd
Granger, IN 46530

The cellar becomes a pocket
in the ground.
Motors turn
and the crane moves away.

Sparrow's song is
indigo evenings
and porch-swing whispers
and pretty paper fans.

Sparrow's song is
a gentle glowing moon,
a cat watching.
Sparrow's song is
bedtime stories
for night's sweet dreams.
Sparrow's song is soft.
Sparrow's song is gentle.